Sevastopol

SEVASTOPOL

Emilio Fraia

translated from the Portuguese
by Zoë Perry

A NEW DIRECTIONS
PAPERBOOK ORIGINAL

Originally published in Portuguese as *Sebastopol*.

First published as New Directions Paperbook 1502 in 2021
Manufactured in the United States of America
Design by Erik Rieselbach

Library of Congress Cataloging-in-Publication Data
Names: Fraia, Emilio, 1982– author. | Perry, Zoë, translator.
Title: Sevastopol : three stories / Emilio Fraia ;
translated from the Portuguese by Zoë Perry.
Other titles: Sebastopol. English
Description: New York : New Directions Publishing, 2021.
Identifiers: LCCN 2020055071 | ISBN 9780811230919 (paperback) |
ISBN 9780811230926 (ebook)
Subjects: LCSH: Fraia, Emilio, 1982– Translations into English. |
LCGFT: Short stories.
Classification: LCC PQ9698.416.R345 S4313 2021 | DDC 869.3/5—dc23
LC record available at https://lccn.loc.gov/2020055071

2 4 6 8 10 9 7 5 3 1

New Directions Books are published for James Laughlin
by New Directions Publishing Corporation
80 Eighth Avenue, New York 10011

Contents

December

Given a choice, I'd never revisit all this. But it happened again today. Watching your video, I was hurled right back into the middle of it. That's why I'm writing you now. Things haven't been easy lately. What happened, when I think about it, feels something like a bandage, something I'm tired of wrapping and unwrapping, as carefully as possible. But it's never enough. I know it's 2018, but I feel like I've lived all these years without actually having lived at all. Like I just woke up one day, bedraggled and over the hill, and someone came up to me and said: Good morning, Lena, welcome to 2038. Or, doubting my sanity, asked: Do you dream often, Lena? And I'd reply: very little. Five years ago, before the accident, I dreamed even less. But Gino liked hearing about my dreams.

Some nights he would sit me down in front of the camera and ask me to tell him about a dream, any dream you can remember. I'd usually tell him the same thing, that I don't typically dream, or rather, that I never remember my dreams. Gino would push and, while I tried to think of something to say so I wouldn't disappoint him, he'd ask me questions about my life, my past, my parents, friends, guys I'd slept with.

One time, Gino came over to my house and showed me one of those videos. It was my voice playing over images he'd shot. Mountains, glaciers, winds across a deserted landscape. I was talking about mundane things, stories from my life, but the way he'd edited it gave the impression that what was being narrated was, in fact, a dream. The truth is, people get bored hearing about other people's dreams, nobody has the patience for that. That's why I don't like to talk about my dreams.

Maybe I'm getting ahead of myself. But your video, the video I watched today, was a little like that. It made me think of Gino, of his experiments with the camera, of me sitting there for ages, rambling on and on. There was something similar about the rhythm, or maybe the tone. But I know it's just another impression, because everything about it was different, too. When I entered that room today, the film was already playing. I couldn't tell if it was at the start or half-way through. The image on the screen, a body on a stretcher—my body, in this case—instantly drew me in. It was a body in the middle of a green room that smelled of urine and medicine. I watched myself lying there, thousands of miles from home, and as much as I wanted to and as hard as I tried, I couldn't think straight. I couldn't move.

I don't remember anything about what happened earlier, the rescue itself, though I was awake a lot of the time. I only know what they told me afterwards, and that I was lucky because I'd been in a section that the helicopters could still reach, which is unusual, search and rescue is always difficult, and every year dozens of people die on the mountain.

The doctor slunk around the gurney like a reptile. He was thin, with something that looked like a wound, a cut on his upper lip. There was a coldness about him, he seemed important. He told my companions that my condition was still touch-and-go and that I would need another operation. They talked over one another, trying to make sense of the situation, sometimes arguing like I wasn't there anymore.

I returned to São Paulo on a red-eye, an evacuation involving both the Brazilian and Nepalese governments, all arranged thanks to the influence of my sponsors at the time. Once I landed, I underwent another surgery and then another, and at the end of it all, I felt like months had passed. My body heavy, in a deep sleep: months, but maybe it had been hours, minutes, years?

This is one of those cases where we have no choice, someone told me, at some point, with his hand on mine—we have no choice but to do what has to be done, do you understand? Then I thought I saw Gino, his face, hovering over mine.

But I want to go back even further.

In December 2012, six months before the accident, I

was at home with a terrible sore throat, drinking tomato juice and watching TV. Sometimes my stamina would take a nosedive from all the training. I felt weak and I remember spending a lot of time like that, drinking tomato juice, with one of those '90s action movies on TV, which for me always had Wesley Snipes on an airplane, a bounty hunter, about to smash through the mirrored windows on some skyscraper.

Suddenly my phone rang. It was Mari. She asked how I was doing, how the training was going, if I was feeling prepared. Feeling prepared. On the other end of the line, I repeated those words—feeling prepared—and then I told her it was all a little weird. I needed a boost, to get back to being 100 percent. Because there wasn't much time left. Before long I'd be facing the biggest challenge of all, I said it like that, I used to talk like that. I was feeling anxious. And I needed to be calm. I was feeling weak. And I needed to be strong. Then she told me she was thinking about getting some friends together at the beach house. She asked if maybe I wanted to go with them. It would be good for me. It's December. Summer's nearly here, there's a warm breeze in the evening.

Even if it's no use now, even if it seems like I'm getting sidetracked, which I'm not, because deep down everything's connected, I think it's important to talk about this trip to the beach with my friends. Remember my frame of mind back then. Think about how things were before.

The trip wasn't all that different from the many I made with Téo, Mari, and the others. But it was the last. That way, with those people.

as soon as the sun stole in, he couldn't stay in bed, he'd get up without saying a word, grab his surfboard, and go out into the water. Wrapped in the sheet, I gave up on sleep. I kept looking up at the ceiling, almost holding my breath, as if I were hanging from a rope, not knowing how many thousand meters high, tottering between nothingness and what felt like the days of acclimatization, that time spent adjusting to each stage of the climb, and each stage is different, that's what Gino told me, what I remembered him telling me, any mountaineer can tell you that the hardest part is the descent, he said, but sometimes just knowing that isn't enough. I remembered him telling me the story of the day Peter Hillary, son of the famous Edmund Hillary, following in his father's footsteps on Everest, reached the summit and made a phone call to the elder climber: Dad, we're on the summit, to which Edmund supposedly replied: great, you're on the summit but now you need to get down.

Gino grinned while he told this story, and I could almost see him. It was as if he were there too, in the bedroom at the beach house, as if I could hear his voice—it was as if he dwelled inside those days at the beach, as if, in spite of Téo, he was with me the whole time.

The breeze batted against the walls, billowing the curtains. I felt hot, cold, my skin shivered, and those scenes kept unwinding, like bandages coming off wounds, or like the compartments of a chairlift at a ski resort, sailing past, one after the other: the common room at a lodge on the way to Everest base camp, Gino drying his boots on top of a yak manure-powered heater; Gino meditating; Gino drinking hot Tang from an aluminum mug in front of a mural with pictures of Sherpas and tourists on peaks like Ama Dablam, the most beautiful mountain in the world.

You probably know all this, of course. Gino was into film, he was a photographer and partner at a production company. He was born in a small town in Italy whose name I could never remember and came to Brazil as a teenager, for his father's job, an engineer. He was almost twenty years older than me. We'd met in February 2011, at a friend's birthday party and, about two months later, we ran into each other again, in a situation some might call unexpected or unreal, because that's exactly what it was. It was my first Everest expedition and there he was, with a team, on the mountain. Gino appeared in a relatively quiet spot, at almost four thousand meters, close to base camp. My team and I had paused our ascent, one of the many acclimatization stops we made that season, and we sat and watched this group with cameras and reflectors in the middle of the snow. There were three of them, plus a couple who I assumed were models or actors. Gino was close by, almost beside me.

We stayed there for a while, staring straight ahead at the bluish glow that fell on the actor couple, surrounded by rock and ice, a scene that, because of the light, looked like it was set against a diorama of mountains and fake styrofoam snow.

Gino gave directions, the actors moved unnaturally, like two little balls of mercury rolling along a block of white marble. When they took a break, I decided to ask him where we'd met. Gino looked me up and down. I took off my sunglasses. He made a gesture of surprise, an Aha! gesture. I wasn't actually sure if he recognized me or not. He called over another guy, who was wearing huge fur earmuffs. I greeted him a little stiffly, and we went back to watching the scene. The couple I thought were actors were struggling not to freeze to death. They wore clothes that weren't at all suitable for the conditions, and all I could think of was one of them having a stroke or getting a finger, ear, or nose amputated, victims of frostbite. But my group soon lost interest. We continued on our way up, to the top, towards Camp One. Several days later, on the long drive back to Kathmandu, I crossed paths with Gino again. This time at the lodge in Gorakshep and, even though everybody stayed there at one time or another, we found the new coincidence funny. We started a conversation that stretched long into the night, with stiff drinks and the cold outside.

Gino told me he was there to shoot a campaign, a series of commercials for a brand of cars—commercials in which cars never appear, he told me, with a pride I didn't understand at the time, but that now makes perfect sense to me.

I told him I'd majored in international relations, but that I'd never really been interested in anything to do with that field. But I finished the degree, more for my parents than anything else. I went through the motions at college while I devoted myself to what really mattered to me. And that's how I put it: what really mattered to me. Which was true, because at that time what really mattered to me were the expeditions, days on the mountain, getting in touch with nature, the thinly veiled vanity of posting a photo at six a.m. surrounded by the ice, some vague idea of isolation and overcoming obstacles.

I looked around and saw my friends trapped inside office buildings, locked in the struggle for a promotion, proud of the fact that they were prepared, efficient, praised by their superiors, proud to speak three, four languages and feeling sure that they'd made it, or were at least on the right track and that ultimately their world was what happened there, between those walls. And as for me, well, I'd found myself, as they say, at an age when hardly anyone knows what they really want. My friend Mari told me that, which is lucky, climbing gives your life meaning, and that's what people really need, Lena, I always say that, people need to believe in something.

At one point, looking out at a suffocating, corny sunset, I told Gino about my project, and that's what I called it, my project: to reach the summit of the highest mountains on each of the seven continents, the so-called Seven Summits. I'd be the youngest Brazilian woman to do it, which, deep down, now that I think about it, was another way of winning, of being admired, of making it. But at the time, this hadn't even crossed my mind. I also didn't think my being there was because my family had money—climbing at a high level is an expensive sport. What motivated me, I thought, was a desire to prove to myself, and to as many people as possible, that I was different, that I could do things that nobody, or almost nobody else, could do.

The year before, I told Gino, I'd climbed Carstensz Pyramid in Oceania. It was one of the hardest things I'd ever done. From that point on, things got serious, sponsors joined, and then I was at Denali and decided to do that first mission to Everest. Because if I was going to conquer Everest's nearly nine thousand meters, I'd need to know the details, see it up close, get a feel for it. The roof of the world, Gino said. Yeah, the roof of the world, I said.

In his armchair, Gino flicked a lighter open and closed. He told me he'd stopped smoking, but he couldn't get rid of that lighter. He kept opening and closing the metal lid with an eagle on it as he told me that he'd also been to Carstensz, that he'd climbed Mount Roraima, and that this was his third time on Everest. The last time he'd taken part in an expedition on the other side of the mountain, which is pretty different from this side, he said. It requires a lot of technique, there's a lot of rock climbing. The rocks are super sharp. If they slice through your down suit, at temps of minus thirty degrees, you only have a few minutes before you freeze.

He said he specialized in films about sports and nature—commercials, TV series, documentaries. Gino waxed poetic about the joys of filming on the mountain. He talked about the difficulties as well. What interested him, he said, was finding new ways to show the same old stuff. He said this with a solemnity, a tone that gave everything a feeling of urgency and truth. He spoke in detail about the work of an artist who'd made a video on the canals of Venice at night, a hypnotic video, he said, a different way of seeing the city, from the canals, at night.

I was paying attention, I liked it when Gino shared ideas with me about how the mind works during a climb. The beauty of climbing is that it's pointless. It has no meaning, it doesn't hide a meaning, it's a person and a wall—that's it. At the time, I liked hearing that kind of thing, I'd even repeat it over and over, like those were my own ideas, and deep down they were, because he seemed to be reading my thoughts. But eventually all that started to sound fake, too.

I remember telling Gino that I had a gray short-haired cat, not a dog, as your video made me believe today. Besides, I've never had a dog, he was the one who liked dogs. I told him I didn't learn how to ride a bike until I was seventeen. Just yesterday, he joked, a stupid thing to say now that I think about it. I said I liked southeast Asian food. One topic flowed naturally into another, but thinking of it now, there was nothing natural about it, and before I realized it I was talking about my mother.

My mother had died of a rare type of cancer that left her blind and wore on cruelly. We were close. In her last months of life, a nurse helped take care of her.

One day I got home, my dad was out, and I found the nurse with his fly down and a hard-on, masturbating just inches from her face and her blind eyes, looking at nothing. It hit me like a ton of bricks. I pulled him aside, told him to get lost, to leave right that minute or I'd call the police—if he didn't leave right that minute, I didn't know what I might be capable of. I never told my mother what actually happened. She asked me a few times about the nurse, she liked him, but I'd say he'd moved to another city and change the subject.

I'll never forget that, I said, and I'd never told anyone about any of this, and I think that's when I discovered that I could tell Gino whatever I wanted. He had an empathetic way about him, and made me feel at ease for some reason. I didn't know it, but I was alone. I had friends, my father, boyfriends, but I was a lonely person.

Little by little, Gino and I discovered shared tastes, common interests. You probably know how good he is at that. During that first trip, on the last night, we wound up banging like two crazed animals. I came four times, the last time he was fingering me, my body clutching his legs, as if I needed his legs, his body, to feel free, and when we were done I started to weep desperate sobs. At the time I was still with Téo. I was sure he was the love of my life, I wanted to have his children, to live with him forever. But I felt like what I was doing was right, like it wasn't wrong.

In the weeks that followed, Gino and I made plans. I said that I'd been recording a lot on my own. I could show him the videos, all of the files, I really wanted to do something with all that footage, I just didn't know how or what. Gino thought it would be extraordinary to collaborate. He had a lot of hours of tape, too. And he could accompany me with the camera on expeditions. We'd do the remaining peaks and then go back to attack Everest. Where it all began, he said. Where it all began.

A series, seven episodes, one for each expedition. A different kind of approach. Action shots, preparations for the climbs, of course. But something more personal, too. Your own thoughts, Lena, stories from your life. That's the kind of thing that really works. Try to show what you're feeling, your stories. He said I seemed to be intimate with the camera. I wasn't shy, that's true. But I wasn't exactly super confident, either. He smiled and, looking at me in that way that seemed to strike right through me, said he thought it could work. As soon as he got back to São Paulo, he'd get in touch with some friends. He knew people who'd be interested in the idea, for sure.

On that first night, the very first, in the middle of our journey back to Kathmandu with our teams, the whole way on foot, a ten-day trek, departing from base camp and hiking past bridges, waterfalls, trees, Gino commented on the color of the ice on the mountain, how it changed throughout the day, in varying shades of lilac.

But now I'm not sure if that really happened. Because in that damn video I watched today, your video, a man was talking about the color of the ice, how it changed throughout the day, and now I'm not sure where this came from, if I'd heard that comment about the lilac color of the ice in the video or if it was something I saw with my own eyes, on the mountain. There was another line about the grayish eyes of the man in the video—you made him look just like Gino, someone ostensibly interesting and mysterious—using turns of phrase and descriptions I'd never say, at least not like that. A smattering of silver in his beard and hair gave his face a metallic appearance and, up close, the strands looked like glittering dots.

I remembered that night. And the others that followed, after we decided to go ahead with the project: train stations and the ferrous early morning air in Kathmandu; Mount Elbrus and the lights of an airport control tower shining through the fog; the month in Aconcagua; our conversations, the ex-wife he'd never see again, the daughter he'd like to spend more time with; my increasingly obsessive desire to climb; hot water bottles in sleeping bags so that, above four thousand meters, our lungs wouldn't freeze. I could hear the ice outside the tent. The ice made noises when it moved or when water hollowed it out from the inside. Gloves, insulators, and socks over socks. Taking care to keep warm, to keep the blood flowing. If we died up there, would the ice preserve our flesh? Or would everything end up gnawed by the wind, until we became dust inside rock?

The truth is, given a choice, I'd never revisit all this, believe me. But it happened again today. At a small gallery, in this city where I came after I decided to take a break, go off-grid, bow out.

Admittedly, I hadn't been feeling well all day. I'd felt dizzy the whole morning, a spasm that started in my right shoulder blade and radiated up to my temple, my blood coursing faster than normal in my veins, making me hold my wrists under cold water from the bathroom tap more than once, wet my forehead, look at myself in the mirror, and listen to my breath.

I had a late lunch, something light and, at around four, I decided to go out. The neighborhood where I live is pleasant, with nice, wide sidewalks. I can get around without anyone's help. There are rows of plane trees, antique shops.

There I was, wandering around, trying to stay calm, when a neon sign caught my eye. It was a bright blue triangle above a set of glass double doors. One of those trendy galleries. For some reason, probably because it made me think of Gino, I went up the ramp and inside. It was a photo exhibition. Even though I'd always traveled lots of places with my parents and visited museums all around the world, I've never really understood art very well. I like to look at it and all, but there comes a point when everything starts to look the same, and I just feel tired. I'd rather wander aimlessly and then get an ice cream.

But today it kept my attention. It was what I needed, I think. Something to give me a boost, something to put me in a different vibe. As I moved through the gallery, there was a series of photographs in a row along the walls. I thought they were beautiful. On the back wall, there were only two, larger photographs, occupying the entire space. In one of them, a light bulb hanging from a ceiling painted bright red. In the other, in black and white, a silver-colored sea under a single cloud. The bulb and the cloud were the same size and seemed to somehow talk to each other.

I was happy I had this thought, how those images might relate to one another, without really being related, but connected by a kind of invisible thread. I thought maybe the events of someone's life worked like that. I lingered there awhile, trying to decipher what those images might be trying to tell me. At least, I thought, my little outing was doing the trick. I'd managed to find a distraction.

I went to the back of the room, where a sort of narrow corridor led to a door, a passageway, protected by a heavy velvet curtain.

Behind it was a small room, in total darkness, with only a wooden bench in the center. A video was playing. Your video. The label said: *The Ama Dablam Route*, and the running time, 42 minutes, just above the name of the artist, a Belgian woman, born in Antwerp in 1984, Nora Pikman—your name, Miss Pikman, your name.

What I can say, my dear, is that I positioned my wheelchair in the middle of the room, the film was playing, I couldn't tell if it was near the beginning or if it was halfway through. A woman's voice was narrating and, against images I thought seemed familiar, she told the story of a woman, a high-performance climber.

As I watched, all I could do was blink, perplexed. This was my story.

My friends, my first encounter with Gino, my relationship with Téo, a ridiculous re-enactment of that last trip to the beach with my friends, the accident—it was all in there, albeit somewhat distorted, and each episode was steeped in this forced, overly dramatic tone, full of over-the-top images. The names, of course, had been changed. And there were unrecognizable moments. There were quite a few. A young female climber, the highest mountains in the world. Watching this, I had one of those sensations that words can't explain, as if the countless times I told my story, in interviews and to packed audiences, I'd been telling the truth, telling things exactly as they happened, but lying. That video seemed to do the opposite.

How could someone have done something like this? How could someone have twisted my story so horribly? Everything in the video upset me. Everything was inaccurate. I don't remember Gino having a lighter, for example. And the whole story about our encounter in the snow didn't happen like that, and neither did my mother's illness, or the night of sex—I didn't come four times, I can guarantee that.

For a moment, I was afraid that everything would be forever crystallized in those scenes. Like a travel diary: when we write in a diary, what we remember from the trip—years later, when we read those words—has less to do with the trip itself than with what we've jotted down in the diary.

I watched the film until the end. It stopped abruptly, in the middle of a stream of thoughts, with the image of a man and a woman crossing an empty avenue at night.

After a brief moment of total darkness, the video started again. It was a shot of a clear day, looking out on a still lake with a few tiny boats leaving behind trails of white foam in the dark blue water, moving incredibly slowly. In the background, a snow-covered mountain. It looked like a postcard.

Ever since I was little, it had been my dream to climb Everest. In 2011, at the age of twenty-one, when I was at base camp for the first time, I dreamed I'd reached the summit.

I felt every sensation: the shortness of breath, tiredness, the happiness of being on top. But I had no idea what any of that really meant. It took a lot of training and willpower to understand and really feel the mountain firsthand. Because above eight thousand meters everything gets really hard, and you feel like you're dying. That's no figure of speech. It's an altitude that causes the body to deteriorate, not just the muscles, but the brain as well.

The worst moments were the ones leading up to our assault on the summit. Five of us made it as far as the final camp: my friend with the camera, Gino Steffe, doctor and climber Max Camargo, the two Sherpas who accompanied us, and me. Then came the problem with the weather forecast ... On Everest, climbers use three weather reports: a British, a Swiss, and a service maintained by the Indian Army. They all said that conditions on June 13th would be perfect. Low winds, mild temperatures, clear skies. But on the 12th, when we arrived at Camp Four, the last one before our summit push, the winds were over a hundred kilometers an hour, the temperature hovered around minus forty degrees.

Nawang, one of the Sherpas accompanying us, was blunt: if you want to go on, that's fine, but we're going to go ahead and dig our graves so we save the others the trouble. We'd planned everything down to the last detail, the idea was to arrive, rest, let the ice melt off our clothes, fill up our water jugs, and leave by eight a.m. at the latest. Because no intelligent mountaineer spends the night in the death zone.

Camp Four is in the death zone, above eight thousand meters. It's called that because anyone who spends too much time there will obviously die. Because of the bad weather, we couldn't move ahead or go back, we couldn't do anything. Sleeping there, without oxygen, was a real risk. So we decided to use the oxygen. Except when the weather improved, we wouldn't have enough oxygen to reach the summit. Not only is oxygen on Everest expensive, it's something we have to carry ourselves. And carrying each cylinder, at that altitude, along with the rest of the equipment, wasn't easy. We went up with

In the darkness, with just a flashlight, around two in the morning, we saw a light. In my expeditions, I'd seen people lose hands, get their fingers, nose, or ear amputated, suffer cerebral edema, pulmonary edema because of the lack of pressure—the lungs fill with fluid, the person drowns in their own liquids—but I'd never seen a corpse.

I thought: now's the time I'll see a corpse, and I tried to prepare myself. From a distance, the light didn't move. We kept walking towards it, at a robust pace, trying to keep warm. Suddenly, I heard a voice, getting closer and closer.

It was a large man, lying with his head stuck in the snow. I tried to communicate with him. In a last-ditch effort, the man lifted his neck: where his eyes should have been, there was a sheet of ice. He screamed in pain. I tried talking to him, but we couldn't understand each other, he didn't seem to speak English, and I didn't speak his language, so we both just stayed there.

I checked his oxygen cylinder: it had enough oxygen for a few more minutes. He was already blind and, when his oxygen ran out, he'd die. A lot of people make mistakes at high altitudes, and there's an unspoken agreement that it's every man for himself. How could I, someone who weighs 60 kg, carry a 90-kg man, eight thousand meters up, and barely able to breathe? I tried putting him on my back so that I could drag him down. Gino told me: Lena, our oxygen is running out, our expedition ends here.

At that moment, a lot of things went through my

mind. One year of preparation. Daily training sessions. Building climbing muscles at the gym. Distance runs and sprints at the park. All of that was going down the drain.

After a few minutes of descent, dragging the man behind us, we saw a cluster of lights. We let them get closer. It was a group of climbers. They were Germans. One of them introduced himself. The man we were carrying was from their team. He had shot ahead and left the others behind.

Now they would take responsibility for the man: his care, his rescue.

I looked at Gino. We were back in the game. I was filled with energy and enthusiasm. We continued at a brisk pace. With so much adrenaline, I had no idea where I was stepping. I hung from the rope about five times. Dangling, rope stretched, with I don't know how many thousand meters below me. We went on and on, not stopping.

On June 13, 2013, at seven in the morning, we reached the summit, Gino and me. Nawang hung back at a distance, showing support. We stayed fifteen minutes at the top. We recorded everything, and I tried to describe the feeling for the camera—at the time, I kept a video diary. Gino got some good shots, we watched the sun rise. Gino hugged me. We kissed. The story might have ended there, but nothing ever works like that.

We started our descent. We were already at Camp One when one of the ropes fixed across a crevasse came loose. An ice pack shifted. I lost my balance and fell. My legs got stuck. It all happened so fast. I felt hot, like something warm had been placed on my knees, something that didn't allow me to think of anything else. While I waited for the search and rescue team, I was sure I was going to die.

Dozens of people die on Everest every season. Search and rescue is difficult. Helicopters don't have access to many sections.

In the ambulance, I had hallucinations.

In one of them, I found myself in the middle of a lawn around an isolated house, flanked by a stream and a row of eucalyptus trees, and I felt a sudden pain. I called Téo and he said he thought we'd better go back. He seemed upset. He'd planned to go mountain biking that day and now this. We put our backpacks in the car and left. On the road, he told me to breathe, relax, he said that deep down it was all my fault: you need to eat better, Lena, eat less meat, do yoga, change your routine, make your body an instrument for expanding and knowing the soul, etc.

He turned on the stereo and scrolled through his phone searching for some song. He stayed like that, looking at the screen, looking at the road, the road getting swallowed up under the headlights, his head moving in a sleepy, blue, sort of phosphorescent way, detached from the darkness like the bust of a statue. At one point, he turned to me and I thought he wanted to tell me something. But he said nothing. He looked back down and kept fiddling with his phone, looking at the screen, then at the road.

Outside, the brush that covered almost the entire shoulder bowed in the breeze, the sky was a puddle of oil, dozing peacefully behind a single cloud, and we were submerged in a feeling of darkness when suddenly something lit up. I didn't have time to turn, Téo looked up, and I think we both saw it at the same time, a blur lumbering across the asphalt in front of us: I screamed and he braked, the wheels locked and the car came dragging to a stop, about two meters from it, now staring at us. The mane. A screech and hooves; the animal ambled off, sluggish—and vanished.

Did that really happen? An animal crossing the road, Téo and I, together, in the car, gasping, watching. In the ambulance, I thought that if everything had turned out fine before, if nothing serious had happened, why wouldn't this be the same? But in the middle of that dream, which I didn't know whether I was dreaming or not, I heard a voice telling me that just because everything turned out fine once, twice, a hundred times, didn't mean it would be that way forever, Lena, all it takes is being in the wrong place at the wrong time, and then a rope comes loose, your crampons lose their traction, a stone shifts from the spot it's been in for thousands of years and that's it. Connected to all those tubes, the ECG machine plotting lines as if agonizing in fear and doubt, I couldn't feel my body.

Through the window, which looked far away, because the roof of the ambulance really did look far away, lampposts flickered past against the night sky, it felt like my face blended with them, the traffic lights on Kantipath

Road and, surrounded by those beams of light, everything was confusing, uneven. The sky looked more like a mirror that reflected nothing.

I underwent seventeen surgeries. Who would ever think that one day you wake up feeling fine, going after your dream of climbing a mountain, and at journey's end a piece of your body simply no longer exists? When asked how he coped, one of the thousands of soldiers maimed in the Crimean War said: the chief thing is not to think. If you don't think, it's nothing much. It mostly all comes from thinking.

In the years following the accident, I went out and told my story. I gave interviews. I did more than one TED talk. I made money. I became a successful speaker, someone who had beat the odds, overcome adversity, and moved forward with her head held high.

I was very active on social media, giving my opinion on subjects that elicited the sympathy of my audience. Many times, I recounted each stage of my recovery, my return to climbing. I began to tell my story in a sincere, transparent, emotionally committed way. The climb. All the tension during the climb. The fallen man. The adventure. The accident. The trauma. The story of my recovery, a year in bed, seventeen surgeries, including plastics, grafts, and others for rehabilitation. The time I went without looking in the mirror. The entire medical debate about whether or not they could save my left knee. Motor and mental confusion.

At first, I would aim my legs, or the lack thereof, toward my father, and ask him for some kind of reaction. I told how the accident had brought us closer together. I told how many times I had the impression that my legs were still there, and instinctively went to stretch them, remembering only at the last moment that they no longer existed. I told about the time I started to cry, saying that the laces on my boots were untied, that I would never again tie the laces on my boots, that I couldn't remember the last time I did. I encouraged people to tell their own stories. You have to break free from all that. You can't keep quiet. Your experience must be shared. People are interested in real stories. You just need to put it out there in a way that inspires.

I'd talk about a former American porn star who'd decided to tell her story. It's touching and genuine when she says how she'd like for society to see her not as a former porn star, but as a mother, wife, daughter. At corporate lectures, I tried to build bridges for topics like personal quests, overcoming, teamwork. I tried to raise the audience's awareness, get them to think about things in a new way and how to apply that knowledge to their routines. This is about me, yes, but also about all of us. People identified with me, and I soon understood that this identification was a key, a key that could open all doors.

Images from the expedition, taken by photographer and documentary filmmaker Gino Steffe, traveled the world. I was honored on two occasions by the Brazilian Excursionist Center. *Reader's Digest* told my story in its February 2014 issue, and *National Geographic*, too: I didn't know my biggest challenge was still to come. At twenty-three years old, I'd suffered genuine defeat. A tough break had radically changed my body, my life.

But I fought back. I moved forward. Happiness is contagious, it boosts self-esteem and strengthens the heart. Make your wish be the inspiration of those who admire you. Crisis is the right time for leadership. In short, don't give up. It was this long and hard path that finally revealed a person I never would have become if I hadn't gone through all that.

In the video, a woman appears from time to time, a woman with wavy hair, a big nose, and thin lips. Is that you, Miss Pikman? She never really looked at the camera but she narrated the story, which, as it unfolded, increasingly resembled my own, and at the same time, was also completely different.

What I think now is that maybe you're an acquaintance of Gino. It's possible you're even close, and maybe he told you all this, down to the last detail.

Or maybe ... and I can feel the blood pumping, I think my head's going to detach from my body, maybe you were behind it the whole time, Gino, and this name, this name, Nora Pikman, is just another invention of your sick soul.

Or is it that, despite all this, everything that happened

today was simply a misunderstanding, a unique coincidence? If that's the case, I must apologize, and congratulate you on your work, Miss Pikman.

One night in April 2017, I was at my dad's house, where I'd moved after the accident, and my phone rang. It was him, Gino.

He said he was in his car, on a dark street in Pacaembu—our secret spot where we used to go to have sex, he made a point of telling me that.

It was eleven when he called, I remember glancing at my watch a little later and it was nearly midnight. On the phone, he gushed with a kind of manic excitement and, at the same time, I think he'd started to cry. He said he'd seen me on a TV show. He said he was happy I was climbing again, even without my—he paused. Legs, I said. Yeah, he said. Then he praised my willpower. He said he always knew my potential. He was proud of me. And he said he'd like to see me. Are you able to get out? he asked. Of course, I said, I'm not dead, am I? I was shaking. He asked me to wait. He'd come by my house. We agreed to meet in front of the garage door. I hung up the phone, placed it on top of the dresser. The house was dark, my dad was asleep.

I went down the ramp, opened the garage door and waited. In the dark, I remember clutching the socket of my metal legs, the cold surface of the straps and buckles that attached them to my body. Back then I still wore prostheses, which I later decided to retire. In the street, the beam of light from a lamppost streaked across the ground. I got a whiff of night-blooming jasmine that reminded me of my mother. I saw the headlights of a car in the roundabout at the end of the block. I saw the window of a house light up.

Leaning against the wall, inside the garage, I looked at the two stumps of my legs. On one of them, they'd kept the knee, which gave the end of it a bigger bulge, a rounded and soft appearance. The other one still had the bandages on, which I constantly rolled and unrolled. How long had it been since I last talked to Gino? I hadn't seen him since the accident. He felt like a stranger, someone from another life, a person who knocks on the door during a storm with his face battered by rain.

At some point, I realized he wasn't coming. I called his number, but no one answered. Over the next few days, I called again, but suddenly there was a message that the phone number didn't exist. Months later, I wrote him an e-mail.

In the e-mail, I said I understood that we might never see each other again. But just the idea that he existed gave me a good feeling, the simple idea of knowing he existed. It was as if a part of me, a part of someone I used to be, was free, walking around somewhere else. But at the same time it was a sad feeling too, because that part of me was no longer mine.

If we ever do meet again, I don't think we'll recognize each other, I said in the message. What if things had been different? What if none of this had happened? I dreamed about you this week. We'd arrived at a lodge, much like the one in Gorakshep. The room was filthy, bug-ridden. You went in first and cleaned it up before I came in.

We're growing farther apart every day, I told him in the dream. I don't know if we'll be able to say these things in the future, because I don't know if I'll be able to communicate with you for much longer. It all happened so quickly. You are the repository of a place in time. I feel like, after so long, the plot of an old movie finally makes sense: the one where two people who like each other very much but can't be together. I remember the feeling of not understanding movies like that when I was a girl. It made me angry. I thought that's the way things were: you either love somebody or you don't. And I remember getting upset at those kinds of movies, the ones that ended with love affairs that only existed in a kind of faraway, elusive place.

The truth is I never sent that e-mail to Gino, or told anyone about my dreams—after all, people get bored hearing about someone else's dreams. But something changed. I started to dislike the person I'd become. Books, lectures, long posts on Facebook. What had I done with my story? To be honest, I did what people do all the time. Tell stories, retell them, freeze them in time, try to make sense of them. This is me, I exist, this is my story, this happened to me, I suffered, I fought, I kept going, I made it, the world needs love and justice, inspiration is the path forward, it's the first step towards making a wish come true. And history is repeated until everything gets erased, and we no longer know what is what.

Whenever I read about people who've died, I think: is this how someone's going to write about me one day? One event explaining another, reasons, motivations?

And if today everything came flooding back, and I now find myself writing this to you, it's because some things never leave us. I don't expect a reply, Gino. But I do wonder: what's the difference between the story in this video of yours and the one I've told myself for so long? Is there even a difference, in the end?

Sorry for going on for so long. Or rather, sorry for being brief, because I know you prefer things that are long and drawn out, sorry for not giving you all the details, gestures, descriptions of anguished characters wandering around and moaning about in the city, smoking a cigarette, or on isolated beaches searching for something that got lost.

In the video, the woman opened her eyes and saw the beach.

From that weekend, months before the accident, I remember banal little things: a sunshade rolling across the sand, Mari walking past in a bikini, a towel thrown over her shoulder, Lóli in sunglasses, standing on the porch, eating yogurt with granola in a blue ceramic bowl. Waves rolling in, neither weak nor strong.

In the end, I think these are things we remember most. We remember a day when we stood by the fire and then put our boots out to dry, or the day we went out early for a walk in the snow and nothing special happened. Would you like to film me telling this? Is that a good enough story for you?

I remember Mari asking me on the porch: Lena, how do you take a shower on the mountain? She'd just come out of the water and was untangling her hair with one of those minty-smelling conditioners that made me feel like I was back home again.

I repeated what I normally said when asked that question. I explained how first we had to go to the lake with a container. But the lake will be frozen over, so when you get there, you have to break the ice, grab a funnel, and fill the container. Then you have to carry that container to the stove. It takes forty minutes just to heat up the water. Then we take something called a shower bag, a sort of backpack with a little hose, a backpack that turns into a shower. The hot water goes inside it. But it's so cold out that water already starts to cool just by pouring the water in there. You have to run as fast as you can to and from the bathroom tent, which is a hell of a long way away, because if you take too long the water gets cold, and if you don't dry off right after the shower, the water will freeze on your body.

Mari, trying to untangle her hair with the comb, said: I'd never make it, no fucking way. I replied: yeah you would, people can get used to anything in situations like that. Then Lóli, who'd been quiet the whole time, said: I don't think we get used to anything at all, not ever.

We stood there awhile, in silence, feeling the sun on our faces. There was a cool breeze. The almond trees between the house and the sea fluttered against the late afternoon sun. At one point, Téo appeared, coming up from the beach, with his board. He came in, closed the little gate. He turned on the outdoor shower. As he wiped the sand from his feet and legs he looked up, he looked at me.

It's getting late, he said, smiling. I repeated: yeah, it's getting late, and I smiled, too.

May

He drags his leg with the bum knee—the worker sprints ahead to shut off the water and turn on the pump. They're the only ones left there, along with a chubby helper who opens up the rooms from time to time to air them out, as they say, warding off the musty smell.

It's a place with rusty cutlery at the bottom of heavy drawers. Chipped cups, chairs stacked atop the stained carpet in the corner of an empty hall.

The fireplace, dark and cold, looks like the mouth of a demon that lost its way, and finding no way back, stayed there, inhabiting the walls, crouched behind each door.

At the back of the patio, a bar sits beside a disconnected hot tub where various items, covered by a tarp, sit forgotten: rackets, shovels, bags of fertilizer, a pair of Le Coq Sportif sneakers with no shoelaces. Around the property, wooden owls dot a gravel path, which looks longer than it really is. After he makes it across the grass block pavers, Nilo stands on the edge of the pool beside his employee.

They watch the water level lower in silence. Nilo smooths his hair, he has white hair. He wipes his hand across his small, blue eyes, afloat on a face that implausibly defies wrinkles. Nilo is wearing a light-colored shirt and the steel-gray windbreaker that accompanies him everywhere, his hands drop to his waist, his fingers reach for the waistband of his pants, he stomps his leg and it locks into his gumboot like a piece of wood.

In the swimming pool, the water leaves behind a dirty ring on the tiles, two feet from the edge. Years ago, when he first got the idea to build all this, he'd imagined a clean, clear, blue basin. But the river water is dark. It gets muddy this time of year because of the rain. His employee's name is Walter. He shakes his head and says this doesn't make the slightest sense; if he were in there, the body would have floated to the top. He says something else. But the pump is hard at work and Nilo doesn't hear him. Walter also doesn't repeat himself. He may well have gotten carried away, Nilo says, had too much to drink, I mean, and fallen in.

If it were a river, the fire department would spend days searching. Because sometimes a body can get stuck on the bottom, tangled up, and won't rise to the surface. That can happen, yes, indeed.

The water creeps down at a tepid pace, and Nilo barely moves, he just stands there, surrounded by the area that was once the campground, the vegetable garden, the orchard. A pine tree rises up next to the white statue of a woman holding a pitcher, and when the wind shifts, the eucalyptus trees on the mountain lean forward, and it is as if they were marching towards the property, gaining ground, and leaving no way out. Nilo blinks and asks when they're going to plant the squash. Walter says they've already planted them, together, two weeks ago. The noise of the water draining leaves him bewildered.

It was two weeks ago. Nilo was on one of the sun loungers, trying to read—an old magazine, with a man catching butterflies on the cover—when he saw the car pull up. It was a couple, they weren't young, the man looked to be his age. In retrospect he must have been younger, but not by much. His name was Adán. His wife, Veronica, was a wispy, nervous-looking woman who wore glasses. At first glance, Nilo thought she was hideous, not necessarily because she was unattractive, though she certainly was, but because she immediately seemed agitated, anxious, restless. She asked if they had a room available. She said she preferred one with large windows because she tended to suffocate in enclosed spaces.

The man, Adán, had eyes that pinched between his cheeks, making an expression that resembled a grin or, depending on the angle, a grimace. He was short, potbellied, with earthy-colored skin and a broad nose. His full head of hair had been dyed dark black. He looked like an old Indian. He said that the day before they'd gone to the wedding of a distant cousin on a farm in Redenção, the city with the dam, the one where the accident had flooded everything. They'd slept there, and bright and early in the morning they'd decided to explore the area, spending the day going from one place to another, visiting stops on the Cheese Trail, touring the local honey producers. Doing some sightseeing, the woman added, which was unusual, since for many years they'd rarely left home.

On the patio, the shadows of Nilo and the couple grew longer, the late afternoon sun carrying them all the way out onto the faded slate pavers at the entrance. This kind of thing still happened from time to time. Nilo apologized. He said that the inn was no longer open. There were eight rooms, separated from each other, cabin-style, and an area where you could camp, but unfortunately the whole thing never worked out. Nilo really was very sorry, because after all these were people who'd arrived, confused, looking for a place to stay, only to find an all-but-abandoned spot in the middle of nowhere, drowning in the landscape, about to get swallowed up by the surrounding wilderness. What he could do in situations like this was offer one of the rooms, even though they'd long sat shut and unused, as long as they weren't bothered by the smell of rotting timber, the ants, spiders, possible cracks, damp corners, and leaks here and there. He could provide clean towels, bedding. Drum up something for breakfast. Something simple. Bread, butter, jam. Juice and milk. Because there really was nowhere else to go for miles around.

Veronica adjusted her glasses: they would clearly not stay be staying. But Adán didn't think it was a bad idea.

He reckoned the man was being kind, and that, speaking for himself, he couldn't bear to drive any further. They'd been driving around since early that morning, and ended up drifting hypnotically along the dirt roads, losing all track of time, traveling further than they would like.

And maybe he thought of it as an adventure, because suddenly he recounted how he used to go camping in his youth, that it had been his dream to buy an RV and travel across southern Chile, that the roadside inns in northern Peru were just like this, bare bones, practically someone's house, but that this was better than a hotel, a thousand times better, no comparison. The woman adjusted her glasses several times. Under the deep-red afternoon sky, their three shadows intersected on the lawn, Adán's flowing from his pair of soiled white loafers, and the woman's head suddenly joining the angle of a potted plant, which gave her shadow a sculpted, extravagant hairstyle.

But that was two weeks ago. Now, the water is dropping, revealing the swimming pool's tiles, and Adán really did disappear, because he's nowhere to be found.

Did you really think he might be in here? Walter asks.

Nilo blinks. He brings up the squash again. He wants to know how long before they'll be able to harvest the squash. His employee replies that if the weather holds, in forty, fifty days, max. He says this and then leans against the railing on the aluminum ladder.

The water is low, the ladder looks like a fragile skeleton. Without the weight, volume, and pressure of the water, it is surrounded only by the tiles, floating, in the middle of the empty swimming pool.

Walter hops down from the third rung. The water splashes up onto his boots, hitting just below his knees. He walks around the pool. He drags his feet along, pushing the dark water. They still can't see the bottom, there's too much mud, and Walter walks around the bottom of pool, glaring up at Nilo, as if to say: this is all a big waste of time, it makes no sense, your drunk Indian-faced friend ain't down here.

Then, for a moment, not even Nilo understands why he asked his employee to drain the swimming pool. He blinks. It makes no sense. There's nothing, no one.

The hours that follow elapse like a long, drawn-out soccer match, stretching on and on. Nilo goes back to look for Adán in the guest rooms, in the orchard, in the small storage shed where there are sacks of feed, cement, a pile of beams. Then he gives up. He falls asleep on the sun lounger, mouth open, his magazine on his chest.

He wakes to a sound. Far away at first, then getting closer. Echoed by the mountains. It's a car, probably a big car, a pick-up truck, driving past the gate at the entrance to the property, its gears grinding. He thinks it might be Adán. He cranes his neck, focuses his attention, and tries to hear something. But after a peak of intensity, the roar of the engine begins to move away. It hangs behind the mountain mist, growing fainter until it disappears completely.

Nilo remembers how, three or four days ago, instead of waning, an engine roar grew louder. Same as all the cars that came down the narrow road at the entrance to the property. The noise grew and took shape. The smell of burning oil filled the air.

Then, coming through the gate and up to the house, he saw a VW Bug. Yellow, well maintained. It gleamed. When it came to a stop and the door opened, a man got out.

It was Adán. Standing there, leaning on the hood. He was smiling. Everything mingled with the sound of the engine, which seemed to percolate inside them—the car was running the entire time, quivering, the landscape trembled, Adán's face trembled, and suddenly the twitch turned into a full-blown coughing fit. Then Adán hawked a ball of phlegm from his lung and spat on the ground, bringing everything to a stop.

He said he'd gone into town the night before. At the bar, he made friends with these two remarkable guys. He'd bought the car off one of them. He bought a little house too. The car in cash. For the house, he wrote four checks. He said all this, grinning, coughing, slapping the hood. Nilo, standing in front of him, blinked. His expression was of someone trying to understand. Someone who asks questions, but isn't getting any answers. Behind Adán, on the horizon, were the mountains and, on top of them, eucalyptus trees.

Nilo remembers this and believes Adán may have gone back into town. Who could say for sure that he hadn't gone back into town, who could say for sure that he hadn't gone to see that house in the light of day? He said he'd bought a house. A place by the river. Or who could say for sure that he hadn't simply grown tired of all this and gone back to São Paulo?

Walter says that could be. It's a possibility. But the yellow Beetle was still sitting on the lawn, behind the guest rooms. I don't think your liquored-up Indian-faced friend could have gone far.

Nilo takes the keys and decides to go to the room. He's still limping, his knee slows his step, it feels like he'll never make it. It feels like it's taking him years, as if, from one step to the next, a long time had passed, as if everything had changed. When he reaches the door, he smells the strong scent of wood, the walls are made of old timber, the room looks like a bunker, in the winter it gets cold and the mist covers the mountain, framed by the window. Adán's belongings are still there. A denim shirt on the bed, boots, socks. His suitcase leaning against the table in the corner. Half a blister pack of pills on top of the dresser.

Things take on a life of their own, that's what Nilo always says. Objects blend with people, over time they come to life.

Not a trace, however, of Veronica's things. Because she'd decided to take off the very first week. They'd had a nasty argument. She'd almost knocked him out with one of those stone ashtrays. You could hear the screaming. She was tired. If you won't change, then how will you ever be free of it? You can stay here with this crazy old man who barely opens his mouth. I'm not going to ruin my life because of you.

So she took the car and drove the more than two hundred and fifty kilometers back to São Paulo. But she called every day. Adán said he had no plans to return. He was going to stay longer. He said it like that, that he was going to stay a little longer. A few more days, a week. He was paying more than what they'd agreed upon for the room, he was feeling good. That's what money is for. It's a kind of energy. Idle money, idle everything. Money flows, everything flows. It was like the fresh air. The river water. But when he told her he'd bought a house in town, Veronica snapped. A little shack for you to take your whores! She said she would talk to a lawyer, scrap the deal, put a stop to it. You bet I will. As for the car, it's probably worthless. You can do whatever you want with it, kill yourself with it for all I care. Adán laughed. Are you drunk again? He said he had enough alcohol to last until the end of the world. Our actions in life are not many. And then one day it's all over.

Before Adán vanished, however, before he was nowhere at all, Nilo had spent a long time with him on the concrete bench beside the tennis court, or what had once been a tennis court. That was the day before yesterday, around four. Walter had seen everything. Nilo sat beside Adán, in front of the frayed net, weeds breaking through the cracks in the pavement. Adán wore a Yankees jersey, white sneakers, white socks. A watch that looked like it was from like another time. He was holding a bottle of whiskey. He smelled like booze.

They sat for a while in silence. The sky was blue. The leaves on the trees changed color as they were carried by the wind and, on the ground, they looked rusty, worn-out. At one point Adán said he would like to tell a story. The story of my life, he said, and grinned, tossing his head back. In the end, old pal, that's all there is to it: people have just two or three stories in their lives. You won't learn anything from it. No one learns anything from any story.

Adán coughed a few times. Then he mopped his forehead and glistening cheeks.

I haven't always had money, old pal. Not that I've got much now, but I've had my fair share of luck in life. He opened the bottle, took another drink. That all started around ten years ago, more or less the time I've been with Veronica—now that was a complete mistake. But what I'm going to tell you happened long before Veronica.

Back then, I had nothing. Sometimes I look back on that time and think: that was a whole other lifetime, which just happens to also be mine, but might not be, because we have more than one life, and they don't all necessarily look alike. Sometimes there's not even any continuity between them, but after a while we learn how to talk about past lives, and they become harmless as we talk about them, and as we start to think we understand what they mean. It calms us down. But of course that's just one more delusion among many. I think that we tell and repeat these stories because we're afraid of them. That's what it is, really. A cry for help. We want someone to help us, to protect us from them.

Adán said that he had been born in Peru, in Lima, the son of a Brazilian mother and a Peruvian father, and that soon after his birth his parents separated, he'd grown up in São Paulo with his mother. But then he decided to return to Peru. It was 1975. I was eighteen, he said. I wanted to know more about my father, who'd died the year before in a fire, a story that had never been fully explained. His car, a red Belina, had been found intact in a vacant lot on the outskirts of Lima. When I returned to Lima, in May 1975, the car was sitting in the garage of his house, where his older sister had gone to live after his death. After some inquiries, which were all dead ends, the car had been returned by the police and no one had touched it since, making it seem like my father might turn up at any moment and get in the car to go for a ride with me around that city covered in dust and people who seemed more like the undead, sprouting up from the dryness of the fuzzy, earth-colored horizons, wandering aimlessly from one place to another.

The car was surrounded by junk, a bicycle, wood-working tools. There was an impressive layer of dirt on the hood. Adán forced the door open, almost breaking off its handle in his hand.

When he settled into the driver's seat, he smelled a mixture of wax and stale beer, which to this day he thinks must be his father's scent. It was what he could believe, and somehow that became the truth to him, that smell, one thing explaining the other, one thing giving meaning to the other. That's how our brains work, right? Adán sat there for a while in the car, the last place his father had been before he disappeared. He put his hands on the wheel. He played with the gearshift. He pressed the pedals.

Break, accelerator, clutch. There was a wadded up washcloth, forgotten between the windshield and the dashboard. A Christmas tree with the words Happy Holidays hung from the rearview mirror.

He regretted that he knew almost nothing about his father, although that's the only thing you can ever know about a person: nothing, isn't that right? I stayed in Peru until 1990. Fifteen years, old pal. There comes a time when everything grows old, too. There was nothing more to do. It was March 16, precisely, the day I went back, the day after you all got a president again, and one month before the Peruvian Congress met its famous demise. A nightmare. It's always the same story for those of us born in this corner of the world, the same story for you all, the same old story, some bigger, darker hole right around the corner. It was a long trip. What did I learn? That there are animals that spend the winter in deep waters. And that with great hope also comes a great lack of hope.

Adán breathed heavily. There was ecstasy in his voice. He told this story and paused. He took another drink from the bottle. He began to babble on about something and grin and suddenly he slapped his forehead, saying he'd remembered something else. He had seen a pig on the property that morning. Lying in the middle of the dirt road. It looked like an ox. It was pink, extraordinary. There was a chunk missing from one of its ears. Must have lost it on a barbed wire fence. It just laid there staring at me, you should've seen it. Then it got up and disappeared behind the bushes.

When he shared this, in spite of all those heartwarming stories of man and animal coming together, tales of great friendship, Adán said he wanted to eat the pig. He smiled. You keep hogs here, don't you? He took another swig. His hands were shaking, clutching the bottle. On the farm, there were half a dozen chickens, one scrawny horse, ducks, a skeletal parrot, which Nilo never got rid of, even though he knew it was wasting away and on the verge of disintegrating into a heap on top of an old wardrobe—but no pigs.

Nilo said he could have pork brought in from town. But Adán wasn't talking about just any pig, he was talking about that particular pig. He smiled. The tennis court was on the upper part of the property. From the concrete bench, you had more or less an overview of the surroundings. There was a winding road, a gentle sloping hill. Behind that, the river, Mr. Hermes's farm, the mountains of eucalyptus trees that looked out of place because they were so tall.

Nilo said he would ask his employee, Walter, to see about it. The pig must be from someone's livestock.

From Hermes's farm, odds are. Hermes's farm is big. A few years ago, his children came in and modernized everything. They started to keep bees, invested in fruit trees, coffee, vegetables. All to supply a chain of stores. They created a chain of stores. Organic produce. Sustainable agriculture. But they didn't once consider giving up the eucalyptus trees. That's where the money was. The old man deals in eucalyptus trees. Has for many years. Little by little the mountains were covered with eucalyptus. If he'd planted eucalyptus, Nilo would have been rich. Nothing he tried to grow really worked out. People said that when Nilo bought the place, he had a wife and a baby daughter. They said he was interested in things like meditation, magic, alternative healing. He wanted to create a community, that's what they said. But then he got it in his head that he could have an inn. He invested what he had, built the little cabins. Then time passed. A long time, nobody even knew how long anymore. It was already like that when Walter arrived. Everything seemed to have happened in another lifetime. Walter often says that it's a region made for eucalyptus trees. Nilo shakes his head, gets angry. Sometimes he has nightmares and wakes in the middle of the night—from a distance you can see him walking around like a ghost, turning the lights on and off around the house.

The story of the pig. The story came out of nowhere and seemed to have no end. Adán gave details about its appearance. Then he spent some time describing recipes for pork. Stews, roasts, pot pies. He said the pig was so fat that his eyes were sunken into his nose. It had a frightened look in its eyes, more like that of a guinea pig. As a matter of fact, the whole time he stood on that road, watching the pig, that's what he'd been thinking about: a guinea pig. One of those little rats, because that's what they are, little rats, balls of fur. The story's actually about a lot of things, but it's mostly about a guinea pig.

Then Adán smiled again, a smile that was constantly changing. He looked down, shook his head, then looked at Nilo: a goddamn guinea pig. Can you believe it, old pal?

Once, he said, his son had asked him for a guinea pig. He must have seen one on some ad or TV show. He asked me with his tiny eyes wide open, two wet little balls. At first he tried to tell Oscar that they didn't make good pets, because they really didn't. In Peru people eat guinea pigs, it's one of those traditional things, which usually shocks tourists, outsiders, like Eskimos who eat live seals for dinner, or the octopuses in Tokyo restaurants that have their heads beaten in and are served up still moving. That kind of thing. One day, if he stayed in that country, his son would also eat guinea pigs. People have cats and dogs as pets, not chickens. Nobody eats a cat or a dog, do they?

Imperceptibly, without the slightest noise, or without either of them noticing the slightest noise, an airplane cut through the sky. Adán put the bottle of whiskey on the ground and rested the palms of his trembling hands on his thighs. Nilo blinked.

They looked like an old man and his demon, and it was hard to figure out who was who. A demon who'd need some help to get home. But it had been a long time, and even if it were possible to return, it would be impossible to know where home was. For some things, it would be better if they never happened at all. I'm talking about death, of course. And how we keep falling, from one ordeal to another.

Adán went to that city to learn more about his father, and he wound up having a child.

Back then, in the early eighties, he lived in a one-bedroom apartment with a tiny kitchenette and a pitiful little bathroom. Gracia, Oscar's mother, lived in a district near Lima called Callao, on a small street near the fire department, two blocks from the Italian sports center, a club for people who'd come to the Americas in search of opportunity, determined not to starve to death, and only managed to fuck up what, for centuries, had already been fucked up by our grandparents' grandparents, old pal. In those days, by day, Adán worked in an office, in a building downtown on Calle Quilca, where the archives of the state department of roadways operated. The door to his office was kept ajar, and anyone walking down the corridor could see him there, beset with maps, files, folders, and reports on what back then was called the Average Daily Highway Volume. Adán was in his early twenties, he didn't have a pot belly yet, he wore his hair long, tied back in a knot, which made him look like an Indian from an old Western, but an Indian from a made-for-TV movie, one who didn't get killed by John Wayne, but by some B-list actor, against a fake desert filled with cardboard rocks.

At the time, I thought things might get better, that the job might lead somewhere, as if a job could lead anyone anywhere, but back then I was betting it would, and so without even realizing it, over time I slowly became part of that room, with those lucuma-colored walls and metal filing cabinets, waiting for the swivel of a fan that didn't really do much, that is to say, nothing at all, against Lima's radioactive heat. Adán took a crumpled photo from his wallet and showed Nilo.

It was of the three of them, the woman, Adán, and their baby son in his arms, in front of an ice cream stand, the Pacific behind them, a place that a decade later would be besieged by a wall of high-rises, with each apartment costing half a million soles or more.

The photo was taken at night and on one side you can see the lights of Callao. It looks like a bomb went off that, in a couple seconds, would wipe everything off the face of the earth.

As for Nilo, he doesn't want any photos on the property. No picture frames, nothing. One day, many years ago, Nilo decided he should leave the photos behind. He felt bad when he looked at them. So he gathered them all into a big wooden box, went down to the basement, and put them under a dresser, pushed against the wall where a rotting oar hung, suspended by two hooks. A place where rafters passed through the damp wall, between old records and stacks of magazines with headlines about flying saucers and lost civilizations. It was as if he were saying to the photographs: stay right there. I don't want you around the house.

He didn't want to find them when he entered a room, he didn't want to see them above the fireplace. In his bedroom, before going to bed, he preferred to be alone with the bare walls, boots in the corner, jacket on the coat rack. It was a simple room. With a bare bulb hanging from the ceiling. A bed that creaked, devoured by termites.

Every so often you could see him through a crack in the door, lying on the bed, masturbating with his eyes closed, in silence, his limp dick in his hands. After he came, a dry emission, Nilo would look at the wall, at the empty shelf. No photos. He'd rather not trade turmoil for piety, old men shouldn't be good or pious.

Nilo looks at his watch, Walter walks beside him. Adán disappeared exactly forty-eight hours ago. Forty-eight hours and thirty-two minutes. He asks Walter if the man might be in the pool. Walter says no. We drained the pool, don't you remember? Nilo blinks. I'd drain all the water from everything if I could! Because water's got a mind of its own. Just like objects. And fire. Nilo had been initiated into Shamanism. He saw shapes in the fire. Fire is linked to clarity and consciousness. Many nights, he would build a fire and sit there, alone, on a log, watching the flames. Man looks at the world through eyes that are circles. The Earth, the Moon, the Sun, and the planets are circular. Sunrise and sunset follow a circular movement. The seasons form a circle. Birds build circular nests, animals mark their territories in circles. Sitting on the concrete bench beside the tennis court, Adán drew circles with a stick in the dirt.

Nilo thinks that men's stories are all one and the same. So when our past is hollowed out, when we free ourselves from it, we can go on to live other lives, find our story in other lives, as if there were a continuum of bodies and minds, and Adán's story is also his story, and also his life.

In Lima, three nights a week, after work, Adán drove a taxi he rented from an acquaintance. It was a Fiat. One of those little ones. He thought about trying to fix his father's Belina, which was still sitting in the garage, but kept putting it off. Deep down, he thought it should stay there, like a fossil. He'd heard his father liked cars. So, every day before he left, Adán stood there, staring at that car. Then he'd go on his way. He would pick up the Fiat at six in the evening and return it around five in the morning the next day.

That week, when this all happened, early one evening, Adán parked behind the Surquillo market, where people go to buy chickens, pork, beef, shellfish, eggs, grain, and fruit. The city's air was poisonous. The last time it rained in Lima, old pal, as I'm sure you know, was in 1940. On the sidewalk, I remember, a blind guy was listening to music at full blast on a battery-powered radio and out of nowhere, I remember it clearly, a mototaxi cut in front of me and a bride and a little girl with an earthy-colored complexion in a yellow dress jumped out, holding a paper bouquet. She must've been about three years old, my son's age.

In the late seventies, Adán later learned, the Surquillo market caught fire and had just been reopened that year, in 1983. Adán thought about how, in one way or another, fires always followed him. This might have seemed symbolic, but deep down, of course, life's accidents can't explain anything, old pal, absolutely nothing. As I recall, it was a market that took up a whole block. Its white walls were painted with lime, and in contrast to the gray of the city, it stood gleaming behind a curtain of soot and pollution.

I'd never been out there before. I didn't know that a man, at one of the stalls in the back of the market, sold guinea pigs. Because that was my mission: to get a guinea pig. It took me a while to figure it out.

On the phone that afternoon, Gracia had said that Oscar was still in bed, and that her mother, an old Indian woman with a craggy face that looked like a crumpled brown paper bag, said we should find a way to get a guinea pig. Gracia repeated this on the other end of the line: that I would have to find a way to get a guinea pig.

First, I thought Oscar had brought up getting a pet again. And I blamed myself for not giving him one when he'd asked me. I thought about how he was sick now, and that it was my fault. Children get sick in situations like this. But it wasn't about that.

I was twenty-five when Gracia got pregnant. We stayed together for the first four months, I wanted to have a family, or at least I believed I did, but one day, I couldn't explain why, everything seemed to fall apart. Or maybe it had never held together to begin with. It was an uneasiness, something physical that I thought would pass, but didn't, as if that formula—the formula of fairy tales, living happily ever after and having lots of kids—now only left me feeling something between dread and indifference.

Then Oscar was born, premature. He fit in the palm of my hand. After his birth, I disappeared for several months. Gracia got depressed, she lost eighteen kilos, I wouldn't be exaggerating if I said she nearly died. Whenever I came around, we'd end up having terrible fights. I'm not proud of it. The boy grew a little, she started to drink, and later ended up going to a support group. I went there one day. I think it was one of the saddest days of my life. It was in this shabby room, lit by bright fluorescent bulbs, with school desks arranged in a circle. Some parents only reconnect with their children many years later. Some parents vanish into the world. Some parents may actually be present, but deep down they're not. They said things like this, which all seemed to be directed at me. The group was sponsored by the church on the ground floor of the building. Gracia didn't show up that day. In her absence, I sat watching one woman. She spent the whole time with her eyes downcast and, near the end of the meeting, she took the floor.

She started to talk about her husband who had died, her son who'd left home, and then segued into a story about the ocean, the waves—it's out of our hands, we have to fight it, but it's out of our hands, on calm seas there comes a time when we get tired of just treading water. Then she went back to talking about her husband and son. And, once more, to talking about the sea. Everyone listened without interruption, hypnotized. The stories ran in parallel, never meeting.

Gracia told me about the animal, I remember, on the phone, in a faint voice, and a silence grew on the other end of the line. She sounded tired.

It was as if Gracia had lost the will to argue and just wanted me to remember that I had a son, and that this son had spent all week throwing up, with a high fever, and had taken a turn for the worse. She said I had to get a guinea pig. Preferably female, less than ten days old. A cuy, from the Quechua *quwi*.

Until that moment, I knew almost nothing about those animals, except that people in Peru eat them, something that always turned my stomach, which seemed more the result of hard times than anything else. At the time, I didn't know the Incas plotted war strategies according to the patterns they found in the entrails of those animals, for example. I didn't know the blood of a guinea pig was sprinkled on the wall of newly built houses to ensure their solidity. Or that old-timers used the animals to heal the sick, to undo hexes, to help lost causes. That's what this was about. Gracia had watched her mother do it all her life. The healer holds the live animal by the paws and rubs it against the bodies of the sick. Then comes a series of chills, sweats. The animal is rubbed against the legs, torso, arms, over the head of the patient. Highly sensitive, the cuy absorbs all the illness from the sick body. And then, at the end, the animal dies. The men cut the animal open from chest to abdomen and examine its organs, looking for anything rotten or injured. And it never fails, it's always there. That's how they determine the type of illness the sick person has. If the animal's liver is bad, it's because there is a problem with the person's liver. If it has a diseased paw, the person's leg should be treated. If its little heart has some kind of tear, the healer has to cleanse the heart of evil and affliction. With a series of prayers and in a sort of trance, a healing treatment is performed on the animal's body. This healing gets transferred to the person and then, at the end, the guinea pig's dead body is placed in a bowl with coca leaves and offered to the spirits.

Walter didn't know whether the stories people used to tell about Nilo were true or not. But he did know that Nilo was a good boss. Even with everything going wrong, he'd never once paid him late. He was relaxed and easy-going. People said he'd been married to a woman, that this woman was young, that she played tennis and liked to swim. They also talked about a daughter. They said that over and over. In different ways. Like old stories from centuries past. There were rumors that over time Nilo had lost everything, that this piece of property was all he had left.

Hermes knew that sooner or later he'd have to sell it. He knew about his problems, about the legal issues. So it would make sense for Nilo to accept his offer. He wanted to expand his farm, his business. It would be better for Nilo in the long run. He was old, he should go back to live in the city. The city is better for old people. Anyway, it was time for his daughter to come back, take care of her father, do something, get him out of that situation.

On the sidewalk, a man hailed the taxi. It was almost ten o'clock. Adán pulled over the Fiat, the man brought his head to the car window, saying he was going to Avenida San Martin, 626. Adán unlocked the back door, the man lugged his big body inside, sat down, slamming the door. He was fat, out of breath. When he saw the cage with the animal in the front seat, he scowled, saying he knew all about this, that it was the kind of thing that made him hate that country, made him hate the whole continent. If you can, my friend, get out of here as soon as possible. Go far away. Here's what the insides of that animal are going to tell you: this is a sick place.

The man lit a cigarette, rolled down the window.

Looking out, puffing smoke, he said the smell of shit in that city was unbelievable. They drove down wide avenues. The man talked about a nagging toothache that was giving him not only a lot of discomfort but also insomnia and a vague feeling of disillusionment. Adán punctuated the conversation with one-word answers, nodding automatically. Out of the blue, the man asked if Adán was from there. Adán said that he was born in Lima, but had grown up in Brazil, that his mother was Brazilian. The man chuckled, shook his head. It's the same lousy story. They're all crooks. Children getting killed every day. Blacks and Indians everywhere. Barricades. The demons have nowhere else to go. A pipe dream. I've been around, my friend. I know what I'm talking about.

Adán turned onto an avenue and everything came to a standstill. Something had happened. He thought it might have been an accident. Then he saw men in helmets. Men working at different points along the road. Craters had been opened up in the asphalt. The car crept along slowly. It was like a glimpse into the future. Yesterday I saw a movie, the man said, about the diesel emissions fraud scandal. Mass murder. Nitric oxide. The automakers turned this city into one huge gas chamber.

Out on the road, the men were melting, trapped by the hot air from the engines of the machinery. They descended, disappeared under the hot asphalt. It was as if there were an enormous furnace beneath the city, with Indians stoking the fires. Taking turns in eight-hour shifts. Logs were stacked in an attached depot, from the eucalyptus trees, from the felled trees. They use the toxic water from the Rimac to control the temperature. The thermometers have to stay at exactly sixty degrees, no more, no less.

It was twenty past ten when Adán parked in front of 626 Avenida San Martin. The man asked him to wait.

In the rearview mirror, Adán could see that something was wrong. The man checked a piece of paper he'd taken from his pocket. The yard at the house at number 626 was covered with weeds. It was probably abandoned.

He went back to the car, got in again. He scratched his head. It's not here, he said. He didn't seem to understand. The cuy stuck its snout through the bars of the cage. It was getting acquainted with the car. It scratched the aluminum with its teeth, causing a terrible noise.

Until that moment, Adán hadn't realized that there was a sort of bundle sitting on the back seat next to the man. He got a glimpse of it and tried to look back over the seat again and saw, poorly wrapped in brown paper, a stone bust.

Sculpted eyes, the head of a statue. The figure of an animal, a kind of brass llama, escaped from its top. It felt like a bad omen. He couldn't explain it.

There being nothing at that address, the man asked Adán to take him back to Avenida Nicolás de Piérola. I'm sorry, sir, Adán interrupted, but that won't be possible. He explained that his son was ill. That he was late, that this was his last fare, that he had to go to Callao and that Nicolas de Piérola was on the other side of town.

The man was silent at first. Then, realizing that Adán was serious, that he really wasn't going to take him, he got out of the car, slamming the door, cursing, saying nothing would ever go right in that shitty country. He carried the bundle with him. As the man waited to cross the street, it became clear that the bundle was nothing more than some hideous knickknack, one of those that adorn the shelves in someone's home, maybe it was a gift, maybe the man was taking it to someone else. Adán then turned around and took the coastal road. He was driving fast. The wires on the lampposts curled against the dark sky and the dim lights illuminated the roofs of the houses coated in dust. On the other side of the avenue, he saw the light from a fire burning behind a wall. A light that moved like the ocean. He saw an acacia planted along the sidewalk and its sad leaves. There was a layer of dust over everything. The windshield was covered in dust. Dust clung to things and people. He thought about his son. He thought he should take a stand, take the child with him, find a doctor, a hospital. The guinea pig was poking its snout through the openings in the cage, trying to sniff something. Adán thought he wouldn't let the old woman cut open that little animal's body, that Oscar would be well soon and it could be his pet. He wasn't sure why, but at that moment he imagined his face pressed against the cold head of that statue. A shiver ran down his spine.

When he pulled into La Punta, he could smell the ocean, the boats, the bustle. Is that where the Spaniards had landed in the Americas? Was that where people disappeared at sea in the seventies? He could hear the little paws of the animal next to him. It was getting agitated, pacing back and forth. Adán put his hand against the cage to calm it down. He made a long, wide turn that seemed to never end. He pulled the car over and, before coming to a complete stop, he saw Gracia across the street, in front of the house, sitting on a doorframe. Oscar was in her arms, covered in a small beige blanket. It was a long night, old pal. Adán prefers, in fact, not to say anymore. A tear runs down his face, it seems more like a wave goodbye.

The river water is darker this time of year. That's the impression it gives. Steadying himself against a rock, Nilo crouches down, fills his cupped hands, splashes water on his face. The river divides the properties and its water is icy cold. It feels like the skin on his face stretches taut when the water hits it.

Nilo is squatting on a rotten eucalyptus log. A log carcass. It must have rolled off a truck carrying lumber from Hermes's farm to the city, to the warehouses, before going to the paper and packaging mills, before being turned into money. Ultimately, that was how money flowed: to the buildings, the airplanes, to vaults at the banks. There are deep and shallow sections in the river. Even in the shallow part it's very easy to drown.

A summer's day, when it seems like nothing can go wrong, bam: a woman jumps in the water, having a good laugh and squealing from the cold. But all of a sudden she gets a cramp, the current is stronger than it looks. Her leg gets caught on a branch. She goes under for a second, then reappears. She waves her arms around, and still it all seems like part of the joke. Then she goes under again. It happens twice more. Nobody else is around. It all happens quickly and quietly. After a few days, the search stops. The fire brigade gives up. The body, gone forever.

He can't ask his employee to drain the river. Nobody can drain the river. He wondered if maybe everything didn't wind up at the bottom of that dark water. He'd be able to see the skeletons of those who've disappeared. They would be green, covered in silt.

Nilo looks up. Ahead, across the river, the lights come on in the house on Hermes's farm. Nilo crosses the bridge. On the mountain, he can see the machines at work, the machines that uproot, strip, and stack the eucalyptus. A mountain is an attempt to get closer to the gods. Like in Egypt, and in many of the desert regions of Central America there were no mountains. That's why the Incas and the Aztecs needed to build the pyramids. To get closer to the gods. The gods, always the gods. In other regions, however, volcanoes made perfect pyramids. The highest ones were chosen as altars, where the Incas took offerings and performed their rituals and sacrifices. The Incas had their own way of mummifying. The ones chosen to be sacrificed were children. Because children were the only ones pure in heart, so they would be entitled to see and speak with the gods. They were the transmitters of information from here to the cosmic world. Some children may have been chosen before they were even born. For those civilizations, it was an honor to have a child sacrificed. It was a powerful thing, in spiritual terms. The process was simple. The Incas went with the children to the top of the volcano. There, they were given a mixture of hallucinogenic plants. The air up high is thin. It's very cold. The children would become drowsy, and hypothermia took care of the rest. Whenever one of these Inca child mummies is found, the preservation of their bodies is astounding. They look like they're asleep, like they could wake at any moment. On one volcano, almost seven thousand meters high, near Santiago, they found the southernmost mummy of the Inca period, El Niño del Plomo. And there are the Children of Llullaillaco, some of the most well-preserved mummies in the world. The oldest is known as the Inca Maiden and she was mummified when she was fifteen. The Lightning Girl, killed at seven, was found with burns on her face from a bolt of lightning that struck her on the mountain. The youngest, called the Boy, was three years old when he was offered up as a sacrifice to the gods of the pre-Columbian world.

Walter says he knows where Nilo read all that, it was in one of those magazines in the basement, right? Nilo doesn't answer. He goes on ahead, walking along the trail. Then he asks about the squash, he wants to know if they've set fruit, if they can harvest the squash.

Are you feeling all right, Mr. Nilo? asks a man in a hat, seeing Nilo standing there, past the gate, now on Hermes's property.

Nilo blinks. He seems disoriented. He wants to know where the pig pen is.

I thought you were coming to talk to Mr. Hermes about your land, says the man. Mr. Hermes said time's running out, that he's waiting for you. You know you can't keep that place much longer, right? The temperature begins to drop. Behind the mountain, the late afternoon sky takes on a peculiar color. Blue, pink. Swelling saplings and branches sway in the air. Translucent, whitish clouds scatter across the darkening sky.

Nilo sees a large man approaching on one of the grassy paths. He wasn't there before, he appeared out of nowhere. The man is pushing a wheelbarrow. When he passes Nilo, he sets it down and wipes the sweat from his brow. His face is dirty. In a real bad way, he says, motioning with his head. At first Nilo thinks the man is talking about him. Am I ill? Is that what people see when they look at me? Then he notices a pig sprawled in the wheelbarrow. It's not moving. Only its dull eyes move. The man looks at Nilo, then at the animal. Gonna have to put it down, he says. He flexes his chest and arm muscles and lifts it again, that mound of flesh, legs slipping over the sides of the wheelbarrow. Nilo interrupts him. Have you seen a man? A man with a face like an Indian? The man lowers his load back to the ground. He wipes the sweat from his brow. Haven't seen anybody, no sir.

In the east, night starts to roll in. The road disappears. On the mountain, the eucalyptus trees bow gently, I think the wind will carry them, I think they're coming. The dead are at peace. Nilo hears a rumble. He cranes his neck. It's the sound of an engine. A car. It seems to tear through the canopy, rising up from behind the eucalyptus trees, climbing the hillside. Echoing against the mountains.

But then the noise seems to grow gradually quieter, fading away. It's him. Adán. He's leaving.

August

At the end of August, I received a postcard. It was a picture of the city of Sevastopol, a soulless port framed by gray buildings, a generic scene, the kind with no story to tell. The card came with a message: Onward, champion!

Of course, Klaus had never been to Sevastopol. He'd bought the postcard online, from some site like easterneuropeanjunk.com. He knew I'd appreciate the gesture. He closed by declaring that we still had a lot of work ahead of us! That was how he wrote, with exclamation marks.

He called me and spent forever mulling over whether we needed to repaint the backstage of the place he'd found. We'd have to do something about the wiring, for sure.

He'd worked out a deal to rent the space for a month, at half price. It was small, on the ground floor of a squat in downtown São Paulo. Poetry readings and musical performances were held there. The other good news was that we'd get to keep all the box-office proceeds, and there was a chance for us to renew the arrangement if our run went well.

Before he hung up, he said that he could come by later

and we could grab a drink at the bar below the overpass, if I wanted. To celebrate. I said yes. I love the beer mugs there.

At the end of the night, Klaus likes to drink what he calls a nice glass of wine and eat a milanesa, preferably in some musty trattoria in Bixiga. About our work, he says, I've got to be practical. Simple things lead to simple solutions, complicated things lead to madness. When Klaus was my age—a lifetime ago, in other words—he was a German teacher. He must be in his sixties, though he looks older. His hair is dyed brown, and he sports a showy, swashbuckling mustache. His teeth are small and jagged, and he's rather thin, especially his face, which is masked in a sickly yellow, his cheeks covered in pock-marks. He always keeps a pen in his shirt pocket. We met at the museum where I work. He used to lead a drama workshop there on Fridays. Staff can take classes for free, and I thought his sounded interesting.

Klaus had just directed a play called *Good Morning, Barabbas*, which ran for a while at a little theatre down on Rego Freitas. I didn't see it, but an actress friend of mine told me that it was awful. Theatre people will flatter you to your face and stick a knife in your back, that's a fact. I got a good vibe from Klaus. In class, I could tell that he knew what he was doing. One day I showed him something I'd written. A story about a mysterious rela-tionship between a man and a woman, set in Moscow in the eighties. The female character had my name: Nadia.

We agreed to meet the next day at a café in Santa Ce-
cília. Klaus arrived on time. He was wearing a tattered
coat and a faded black shirt, which gave him a penurious
appearance. He ordered a coffee. I ordered a mint tea.

He said something about the museum, how poorly the
instructors were paid, and that it was unlikely he would
continue teaching there. They're a horrible bunch of
people, I said. I worked for the museum's educational
program, leading guided tours for school groups and
young people. Other than the girl with the shaved head
who worked the cash register at the gift shop, there was
nobody there I really liked. My boss spends all day posting pictures of artwork on Instagram, you know? One of
the guys who works with me is involved in cultural production—grant-writing, setting up projects—and he's
an artist himself. His work combines photography and
installation, and seeks to discuss inequalities in the art es-
tablishment, to draw attention to historically overlooked
groups. It's a collection of photos of concrete barriers,
and none of the things he says his work is about are actually *in* the work, which really pisses me off. Anyway, I
guess I'm kind of pissed off about everything—my dad
told me that, actually—so maybe I'm being unfair.

Klaus grinned, coughing, he put a handkerchief to his
mouth. Then he opened a small, crumpled pouch of to-
bacco and began to roll a cigarette. He got straight to the
point: he was looking for someone to help him out. He
wouldn't be able to do all the research for the play he was
starting to write, and research was the most important
part. I disagreed. Research matters as much as, I don't
know, a cherry, I said. A cherry in a cocktail. A cherry

in a cocktail after two in the morning. Anybody who's not a complete idiot knows that there should be only one cherry per drink and that the cherry's only there so that it can be removed. I was being serious, I meant it, but Klaus was amused by what I'd said. I told him that what I was interested in was writing, but I might be able to give him a hand with his research.

He looked at me, sat quietly for a moment, and then assured me that I'd get to write as well. Depending on how things worked out, I might even get a credit as his cowriter.

I didn't believe him for a second, but, on the other hand, it didn't seem so far-fetched. I realized then that Klaus was a lonely person. He had no money and no friends, and couldn't count on many people.

He had done political theatre in the seventies, which was when he'd made a name for himself, or, rather, a name among theatre buffs and writer friends, which, fair enough, is still something. My dad always says I shouldn't be so critical. But since then Klaus had kept to himself. I got old, he said. The world changed. I've never been part of the in-crowd, and now I'm paying the price. Klaus had spent the past few decades putting on shows for virtually no one in grungy theatres downtown. But he was happy that way. You can only be happy that way. He took another sip of coffee, and then he rested his hands on the table and began to tell me about the play he was writing.

It's a historical play, he said. It takes place in 1855, in Russia, during the Siege of Sevastopol. I pretended to know what he was talking about. It's about the life of a painter, Bogdan Trunov, a man who reached his hey-day during the war years and then died young. He left behind many paintings, which have only fairly recently been discovered. What's most fascinating, Klaus said, is the way Trunov was always breathing the leaden air of war—he was up to his neck in it—but war, the war itself, never appeared in his paintings.

I left my job at the museum and went to work for Klaus. He didn't take it very well when he found out I'd quit. I told him that I would have done it anyway, that it wasn't because of him. I just didn't want to be stuck in that place anymore. I'm not paying you a penny more, he said. Klaus paid me peanuts, no question, but I had some savings and could get by. Anyway, it really wasn't because of him or our play that I'd quit my job, I repeated. That was how I put it: *our play*. And Klaus laughed.

He could laugh, I have to say that. It was something I noticed right away. He laughed with his whole face, and with his shoulders and his arms. I was thinking later about the complex motions involved in laughter. It's all so weird. Opening your mouth, showing your teeth, producing sounds, rocking your body. No matter how fucked up humans may be, they still want to laugh. You can't show sadness by simply presenting a man who's been trampled on and screwed over. Deep inside the eyes of a sad character—someone who's really been tested by life—we must also see hope. Klaus said things like this, and I wrote it all down, absolutely all of it, in my notebook.

*

At night, Klaus would take me to the bars on Vieira de Carvalho. Drunk, we'd roam the streets of República, along Avenida São Luís, past the gray boulevards, the tangled nests of wires on telephone poles, the guys giving blow jobs in dark alleys, the statue of an Indian whose shadow bore down on the transvestites who gathered at Largo do Arouche to smoke joints. Sometimes we stopped and smoked with them.

Then we'd head to Nove de Julho, where Klaus's apartment was, on the fourth floor of a building with dark hallways and a doorman who resembled a zombie, sitting behind a little wooden desk on the ground floor. The apartment was stuffy and looked like a room in Count Dracula's castle. A green light blinked in the street below the only window. There was a steady, electric hum that made the couch, the stained carpet, the smell of cigarettes and of old food in the fridge seem all the more gloomy.

I think it was because I'd just been dumped by my boyfriend and didn't have anywhere else to go that I spent so much time with Klaus. My dad said I needed to get a real job, but that's what parents always say. Some nights I slept at Klaus's place, on a foam mattress in the living room. Before I fell asleep, he'd tell me about the guys he'd seen while cruising the streets, or at bars. When he liked a guy, he would remap his routes, hang out at the places where the guy liked to hang out, often sending himself on a kind of wild-goose chase, which he would recount to me in detail.

He described the clothes these men wore, their hands (Klaus liked hands), their gestures, the bulge of their dicks in their pants, he told me if they were tall or had a beard. The flavor of the month was a little blond actor, who, he said, was just what we'd imagined for the hero of our play. A gorgeous queen. He said that he wanted to introduce me. To see what I thought of him, because we had similar tastes, he said. He could not have been more mistaken.

In the morning, Klaus and I would wake up and have breakfast together at a little dive on Martins Fontes. I'd order orange juice and buttered toast. Klaus would have a glass of cold milk. Then I'd spend the rest of the day organizing research files and reading about nineteenth-century Russia. When the clock struck five, I'd start writing my own stories and draft scenes for the play, and every once in a while I'd jot down what I remembered from my dreams the night before. When night rolled around again, we'd go out for a drink or take a hit of the acid that Klaus kept in a plastic sleeve with his driver's license, and then we'd sit, paralyzed, on the couch in front of the window, looking out at the city. Once the acid eased off a little, Klaus would rave wildly for hours. He'd rant about the play and everything he imagined for it, and brainstorm solutions to production problems, motivations for the characters.

Whenever he talked about the blond guy, the one he thought would be perfect for the role of Trunov, he said that he was sure I'd like him. I saw him in a play a while back, he said. He's got talent, not just a pretty face, no—

he's really good, believe me. Yesterday, he went on, I took the bus with him. I rode all the way to the last stop, in Santana, can you believe it? I had no reason to go all that way, of course, but I pretended I was going to visit an aunt and sat down next to him and we got to talking. I couldn't stop looking at his hands—they were firm but soft, with pink, rounded nails. I looked at the hair on his arms. We didn't talk about sex, of course, but I can tell he loves it. I can pick up on that sort of thing. Now, whether he's a good lay or not, I wouldn't know. The problem sometimes is that even people who love sex are scared to death of sexual fantasy. A lot of folks, if they could, would put an end to sexual fantasy, because that's what carries us through life. Then Klaus repeated for the thousandth time that the guy was perfect for the role, that he'd give Trunov the strange and distant quality we'd imagined—of being and not being at the same time.

An eccentric quality, for sure. Unlike his fellow wartime painters, Trunov had no interest in the battlefield. Or, rather, he had an interest—those were the times he lived in, after all, and it would have been impossible not to express that in some way—but it wasn't the kind of thing he wanted in his paintings. The ranks of soldiers in the field, the cavalry with flags raised. He didn't capture the upheaval, the triumphant generals, the human suffering. Instead, he focussed on the soldiers' everyday lives, when they weren't at the front: the little breaks, the downtime when nothing was happening, soldiers with grubby faces waiting to hear the whereabouts of their artillery batteries or playing cards at a staging post.

*

Something else I learned was that Trunov—born in 1818 in the city of Odessa, died in 1860, at the age of forty-two, a man Klaus described as full of energy and self-respect—had very particular methods when it came time to paint. He didn't do full-scale studies for his paintings, for example. He did almost no studies. He had the habit of starting his sketches with no plan in mind. He used to paint figures and set them aside, then arrange them against backgrounds he'd prepared separately. So, even when the figures interacted with one another, the connection between them seemed unnatural. Their eyes, Klaus told me, almost never seemed to meet, which gave the paintings an unusual psychological dimension and a dreamlike ambiguity. In one of Trunov's most famous paintings, some soldiers play chess with pieces made from scraps of bread. In another, a lieutenant dozes atop a white horse, looking like he's about to fall off. In another, soldiers talk, or seem to be talking, while a plump woman holds a colorful feather duster.

From 1854 to 1855, when Sevastopol fell, Trunov lived in neighboring Simferopol. In 1855, while the Russians were losing up to three thousand men a day, Trunov spent about four months shadowing a regiment. He nearly died more than once. He did this on his own, spending his inheritance, because joining the war voluntarily cost money. It was a very prolific period for him. One of his first paintings from that time shows two soldiers, surrounded by smoke, sitting on the stones of a collapsed wall, eating watermelon. One of them is slicing the whitish melon with a pocketknife. They appear to be talking, but most likely, Klaus says, they were painted separately and then mounted against the background of the canvas.

One morning, while we were eating breakfast, I told Klaus that I didn't quite understand why he was writing a play about Trunov. You like the guy's paintings, I said. There's something about them that moves you, fine, but it's just a weird story where nothing happens.

Cars streamed past in the street outside. Klaus wiped milk from his mustache with a napkin and said that all stories, at heart, were weird stories where nothing happened. We are the past, he said. I said, no, we're the future. He laughed at that. I asked him to explain what was funny. He said no, he wasn't going to explain anything to me. And, besides, it wasn't true that nothing happened in the story. He was just now working on a very rousing scene.

A very rousing scene, I repeated.

Yes, he said, a very rousing scene. A very rousing scene in the life of Bogdan Trunov.

Klaus and I had got drunk the night before and were trying not to die. My head was about to explode. It was a cold, sleepy morning. We were sitting in a sheltered part of the café, away from the draft. He wore a scarf with a brown moose on it that matched the color of his mustache. I ate my toast, looked at Klaus, and thought that, if anything was weird, it was my life.

My parents lived in the countryside, and whenever they called I'd say that things were going well—my job, school. I'd tell them about mundane stuff, like when the microwave broke and I had to get it fixed. I made up a story about meeting a new guy, who was very smart and had a job. To be honest, I wanted to be able to tell my parents that I'd gone through a terrible breakup, that I'd dropped everything and was working with a famous director on a play—I mean, they wouldn't have had a clue who he was, of course, but I'd explain that Klaus was a famous director, a visionary genius. I was just waiting for the right moment to say it. I came close several times. But the months passed and I said nothing. When it was all over, when the play debuted, I'd have my revenge, I thought. They'd tell me that I was right and forgive me for everything. I ordered a mint tea. My head felt detached from my body.

Klaus went on to tell me about this rousing scene, which, of course, was far from rousing, because what Klaus liked was anything but action. He liked what he called the lingering moments: the rain, dunking cookies in milk—that mustache dripping with milk was disgusting. And, of course, he liked lunatics and lost people.

One day, Klaus told me how, in horror stories, mysterious characters suddenly appear, wearing clothing from centuries past, as though they'd been asleep for years—or for eternity, which is one and the same—and then suddenly awoke and knocked at the door, hungry for blood.

That was exactly what would happen in our story, according to Klaus. One morning, a man would knock on Trunov's door. Not at night but around midday—

which, ultimately, I thought was a good idea, not at all clichéd, everything happening at the brightest hour of the day.

The man stands waiting in the doorway. He is a soldier. His face is grubby, and he doesn't look more than thirty. What's remarkable about him, Klaus said, as though he weren't making the whole thing up then and there, is his white hair, a contrast with his youthful features, his thin, ruddy face. A handkerchief is tied around his left wrist, and he wears a dark uniform, patched at the knees. His tattered old coat, adorned with an insignia, looks to be the finest garment he owns. He might even be handsome, he said, if it weren't for his overall look of exhaustion, the crisscrossing expression lines hardening his features. Are you Mr. Trunov, the painter? he asks.

Standing halfway between the door and the kettle on the fire, Trunov looks at the soldier, who waits behind a curtain of dust, backlit by the pale sunlight. He invites the soldier in. I have a request, the soldier says. I want you to put me in one of your paintings. Trunov takes a few steps back toward the fire and stays there for a while, looking at the flames, looking at the man. He warms his hands. He takes a sip of water from a shiny cup. He wipes his mouth on the sleeve of his dark sackcloth coat (this was a detail I'd researched, which Klaus was now using and, you've got to admit, it's what gives the scene its charm). The soldier's gaze hovers over the silver candlestick on the table, the clock on the wall with the picture of Peter the Great (me, again), and the stack of firewood, before landing once again on Trunov, whose answer takes a little too long to come (we'd have to fix that later).

Trunov thanks the man for his visit and his interest. He says that he can certainly paint him, but this is something new, it's unusual for his subjects to approach him. He usually goes out in search of people willing to pose.

After a brief silence, and realizing that the soldier isn't going to say anything more, Trunov asks him how he would like to be depicted.

Here Klaus said he'd imagined an elaborate and perfectly steady play of light. He wanted the moment of hesitation between Trunov's question and the soldier's reply to stand out, as if it were something solid and heavy, something we could feel. The soldier would stand there in silence, stare at Trunov, then say: in the midst of battle. Among my fellow officers. I'd like to be in a trench or on horseback carrying a flag. With the enemy fleet in the distance, the white batteries on the shore, the aqueducts, clouds of smoke, the wind in our faces. On the horizon, enemy fire.

The consciousness of solitude in danger, Klaus said. That's the feeling we've got to strive for. Are you writing this down?

He stuck a piece of bread in his mouth and took a sip of milk.

I asked whether Trunov would agree to do the painting in the end.

Yes, of course, Klaus answered. That's the event that will propel our story forward. He lowered his head with a sad look on his face. But Trunov will not accompany

Deep down, I didn't really like him. I kept trying to figure out if I really liked anyone. I liked Klaus, but that was different. I thought about the big picture, about my generation, crushed by another ten, fifteen years of paralysis. I thought about how I should have studied economics or, I don't know, software development, artificial intelligence. At my age, I should have been inventing a new technological paradigm, building robots, making money. But no. I went back to the story I'd been writing. About the mysterious connection between a man and a woman.

Now the story took place not in Russia but in a dreary town on the southern coast of Brazil, a town with gusty mornings and white skies, with shops selling beachwear, floaties, Styrofoam boogie boards. Nadia, from the single lighted window, waves at Sasha. She's in one of those squat, low-rise buildings slowly eroded by the salt air. Sasha, who is waiting in the courtyard, sees the apartment light go out. Then a door slams, and he hears footsteps on the stairs, at first distant, formless, with lulls between floors. The clatter of keys, the gate, and then Nadia approaching. She has a letter. She gives Sasha instructions. Propped against the little gate, he looks at Nadia. It's always possible to go crazy when you're alone at night. In the courtyard, Nadia feels like she's being watched, and she could swear there's a device in her chest, some sort of mechanism, going tick-tick-tick. She points to her chest. You know the story of the crocodile that swallowed the alarm clock? A leaden air descends on them—silence. Nadia glares at Sasha. He bows his head. She hands him the letter and turns around. Sasha hears the gate slam. He stands there for a moment, think-ing about the debt, because Nadia, what little she said, insisted on this—a debt that Sasha will have to pay back sooner or later.

Nadia's orders were for him to make his way to the pier in front of the Italian Club, drop the letter on the curb, and leave. And never look back. Like in a detective movie. The sea is smooth and glassy like a dish of milk, and at that hour no one else is by the water. Hulls bob up and down in the dark, the club's neon sign blinks on. And off. On, off. Sasha wipes the sweat from his brow and sits on the curb. He fixes his gaze on the water. The next day he will have to obey Nadia again. And again, and again. Because he's settling his debt, which he can't understand. One day you'll remember, yes: when Nadia said that, her lip trembled.

I think deep down I wanted to believe that Sasha and Nadia could be friends, could stroll through a strange city together. But I couldn't write it that way. This filled me with irreparable sadness. I glanced at the pathetic bookshelf in my living room, at the wooden bowl filled with pencils, paper clips, Post-its, a sushi-shaped eraser, a little plush monkey that had been a gift from my mom. I looked at the only picture hanging in my apartment, a tiny student apartment. It was a pitiful little landscape, with a big white mountain.

The next week, I went back to my meetings with Klaus. When I got to his apartment, the door was ajar. A song wafted from inside, some tune from the seventies that I couldn't identify. Klaus was waiting for me, smoking, a map open on the kitchen table. He looked even thinner than usual, as if he hadn't slept in days. He showed me on the map where Sevastopol was. I told him that I knew where Sevastopol was. He ignored me and kept pointing at the map. Sevastopol is a port, he said. It's a funny name. This is the Black Sea. Minerals make the water dark. It's what they call an inland sea, because it's surrounded by the mainland. It's connected to the Atlantic by various stretches of water, but, if you look at the map this way, the sea looks like a big hole. Or, rather, a drain, in the middle of the map, where the whole world will get flushed away.

Klaus ran his hands over the map, unrolling it across the table. And this is the world, he said, and laughed.

I heard the click of the turntable in the living room; the record had ended. Klaus sat down. He said he had something to tell me. I expected the worst. He was silent. Then, as if he'd suddenly swerved around a bump in the road, he started talking about the blond guy. He said he'd run into him a few days ago, at a friend's birthday party, in a nightclub downtown. When the booze had all been drunk, the party had migrated to a bar. Then another. Klaus had followed him all night. When he got the chance, he talked about the play. We were very drunk. I ruined everything, he said, laughing in a way I'll never forget. He's no longer on the project. We'll have to find another actor. Klaus laughed again. He laughed and seemed to be crying, too.

Suddenly I realized that Klaus had aged since we first

began meeting. The wrinkles, the white roots in his thinning hair. He looked fragile, weak, his eyes hazy, coated in a gooey yellow film. He'd been drinking too much. He always drank. But it had got worse. There was something inscrutable about him, that was my feeling—a tumultuous heart, in which nothing was clear-cut.

To break the silence, I asked about Trunov, whether Klaus had worked on the play in the past few days. Barely, he replied. To tell you the truth, Trunov has taken a lot out of me. He shook his head as he said this, and winked at me, a sad, almost involuntary wink, as though he were seeking some kind of accomplice in his sadness.

Trying to cheer him up, I told him that I'd managed to get someone to look into the theatre's wiring. He'll take care of everything. He'll paint the stage, too. The lighting will be perfect. It's gonna work out. I don't think the stage is small. It's the ideal size.

I opened my backpack and pulled out a stack of printed paper held together by a rubber band, with notes in the margins. These are suggestions, I said. I'd like you to read it. I thought a lot about Trunov, our story. It's going to be a great play. I pushed the pages toward Klaus. He held them limply, then set them down on top of the map, just above that city with the funny name.

What I had in mind was that Trunov wouldn't be able to paint the picture.

He'd assemble the fake battle scene. But he wouldn't be able to do it. He'd throw out several attempts. And, instead of the battle scene, he'd paint another scene, something quiet, a simple portrait of the soldier in his tattered uniform, the one he wore the day he appeared on Trunov's doorstep asking to be painted. The soldier would be standing in front of a staging post, his face unexpectedly lit up by a crooked smile.

Trunov takes his time with this painting. He wants everything to be perfect. The days go by. But, before he can finish the painting, he is surprised by news of the soldier's death. A bomb in the trenches. It happened quickly, the way death often does.

Trunov mourns the young man's death and sets the painting aside, unfinished. The frosts come and time passes and everything ends and begins again. Summer arrives and, with it, the end of the war. The soldier's portrait will be lost for decades, until the mid-nineteen-sixties, when it's discovered accidentally by a collector, in an antique shop in Siracusa, Italy. A series of investigations confirm that it is indeed a work by the Russian painter Bogdan Trunov. And only at the end of our play do we find out that this collector, a lonely man with gray eyes, is the narrator.

We debuted two months later. The play was a flop. Everything sounded fake. The script didn't work. Nothing worked.

The actor Klaus picked, another strapping, angel-faced young man fresh out of some crummy drama school, was dumb as a post. He couldn't understand a word he was saying. The actor who played the soldier was a little better, but he wasn't convincing, either. The lighting was great until halfway through the show, when everything went haywire. My parents made the trip into the city, and at the end of the performance I think they just felt sorry for me, because my dad took out his wallet and handed me two hundred reals. Don't forget to eat right, dear.

During the month the play ran, the audiences who used to come to the squat to see gigs and poetry slams— poems with positive messages that spoke of love and trauma, loss and abuse, strength and overcoming—simply evaporated. We weren't able to renew the contract with the folks who ran the cultural program there, and we buried the story of our play.

On the last night, after the performance, I went with Klaus to a trattoria in Bixiga. I was devastated. He was tired but seemed happy. He ordered a glass of wine and a milanesa. I ordered the gnocchi. We barely said a word about the play. Klaus quickly got drunk and started talking as if he'd never stop. At one point, he began to tell a story about Giacometti, the sculptor, a story I found eerie and sad. In 1914, he said, when Giacometti was just thirteen, he sculpted a head, the first head he ever did from observation. His brother was the model. It all turned out fine. But, fifty years later, he spent nearly a month in his studio trying to recreate that first head, the same head, same size. But he couldn't do it. It never came out the way it had the first time. Suddenly, everything was a mess. If he looked at the head from far away, he saw a sphere. If he looked at it up close, it was something much more complex. If he looked straight on, he forgot the profile. If he looked at the profile, he forgot the face. Too many levels.

As Klaus spoke, I listened to a man who was singing and playing a Casio keyboard. One of the songs was about an *emergenza d'amore*. "And I will carry you/ In my pockets wherever I go/ Like a coin, an amulet/ That I will cradle in my hands." I sat there listening, my eyes red from the wine. The room seemed to ripple, with its twinkly lights and photos of actors and actresses (Marcello Mastroianni, Sophia Loren) and colorful ribbons dangling from the ceiling. When the song ended and lifeless applause sprang sporadically from around the room, Klaus said that he was leaving. That was how he said it: I'm leaving. I didn't understand what he meant. Leaving to go where? He was drunk. He apologized to me. He tried to look me in the eye. Will you forgive me, Nadia? I can't stay. I hope you understand. I can't stay any longer.

Even today I can't explain it. Goodbyes are like that, quick, and we never know when they'll actually happen.

That night I left the restaurant and walked to the Brigadeiro metro stop. It was cold, and the city looked like a giant space station, a forgotten corner in the vastness of the heavens.

I remember, when I got to the station, taking a while to find my metro card in my bag. Then I put my headphones on. I went down the escalator. It was late; there was hardly anybody on the platform. Sitting on a bench was a dirty homeless man. He moaned; the corners of his mouth stretched to show his teeth. The man was hunched over, trying to keep himself warm. He looked at the ground and rocked gently back and forth. I opened my backpack and pulled out an old sweatshirt. I placed it on his lap, feeling a little ridiculous.

Soon my train arrived. That night, I stayed up writing almost until morning. Once again, the story began with Nadia waving from the single lighted window, at the top of a low-rise building. But I changed just about everything else. Instead of Moscow or a seaside town, the story was now set in the city of São Paulo, in a sufficiently distant future. There were no more secret letters. Nadia and Sasha were older, too.

Sasha stood waiting in the building's courtyard. He was just dropping by to visit Nadia. They were friends who hadn't seen each other for a long time, or maybe they had once been a couple. She said that she liked living on the top floor, in the highest apartment. The building used to be taller, she said. Many years ago, during the siege, a bomb took off the top. A Chinese tailor lived on the ground floor and took refuge there—he couldn't leave. Today, the tailor's family owned the building and rented out the apartments; the price was low and the street secluded.

Sasha and Nadia walked down the block to a sort of

bar with a big window, on the top floor of another building. At first it appeared to be a residential building; there
was no sign, and no noise could be heard from the street.
In the dark, they climbed the stairs, turned down a corridor. A door opened. They entered a smoky room with
a bar and people drinking and talking so quietly that you
couldn't tell whether they were real people or just pro-
jected images. The window looked out on an overpass
and a compact cluster of buildings and lights. There was
a red ball in the sky. Nadia told Sasha about a trip she'd
taken many years ago, when she was still a child, to the
house of some friends of her parents. It was the first time
she'd ever left the walled side of the city. Everything
was new. When she arrived, she was given gifts: a doll, a
seashell, a music box. She'd never seen anything like it.

Later, she would tell Sasha the same story again.
I don't think she realized that she was telling the same
story. People always tell the same stories, even when they
try to tell new stories. Stories are laid out in front of us,
like objects, and over time we realize that they're all made
of the same material, a solid mass of stone and metal.

Nadia told the same story at dawn, as she and Sasha
tried to cross a wide avenue. For a moment, she seemed
to catch a glimpse of herself from the outside, like an
image beside Sasha. They continued down the avenue,
which grew wider and wider and impossible to cross.